Say "Cheese!"

by Christine Ricci
illustrated by Steven Savitsky

Ready-to-Read

Simon Spotlight/Nick Jr.

New York   London   Toronto   Sydney

Based on the TV series *Dora the Explorer*® as seen on Nick Jr.®

SIMON SPOTLIGHT
An imprint of Simon & Schuster Children's Publishing Division
1230 Avenue of the Americas
New York, New York 10020
Copyright © 2004 Viacom International Inc.
Manufactured in the United States of America
First Edition
2 4 6 8 10 9 7 5 3 1
Library of Congress Cataloging-in-Publication Data
Ricci, Christine.
Say cheese! / by Christine Ricci ; illustrated by Steven Savitsky.— 1st ed.
p. cm. — (Ready-to-read. Level 1, Dora the explorer ; 5)
Summary: To cheer up Boots the monkey who is sick, Dora and her animal friends make
him a photograph album. Features rebuses.
ISBN 0-689-86496-5 (pbk.)
1. Rebuses. [1. Photography—Fiction. 2. Animals—Fiction. 3. Rebuses.] I. Title. II. Series.
PZ7.R355Say 2004
[E]—dc21
2003007583

Hi! I am  . My friend
DORA   BOOTS

is sick today.

How can we cheer him up?

I know! We can visit

BOOTS

at his  .

TREE HOUSE

And we can use my

CAMERA

to take pictures of things

 likes.

BOOTS

would love a picture

BOOTS

of and .

BACKPACK   MAP

Say " !"

CHEESE

We are at Mountain.
STAR

 Mountain is filled
STAR

with .
STARS

 loves to play with
BOOTS

the !
STARS

Look! There is .
 has all kinds of .

TOOL STAR

TOOL STAR

TOOLS

Say "  !"

CHEESE

Here is a fruit garden.

Which fruit does  like?

Yes, BOOTS loves BANANAS !

Who else loves ?
BANANAS
The !
BIRD
Say "!"
CHEESE

likes silly things too!

The are making silly

faces.

Ha, ha, ha! Smile,  !

CROCODILES

Say "  !"

CHEESE

Do you see more silly things?

has baked a

ISA   CAKE

for .

BOOTS

Yummy!

made a for .

BENNY   CARD   BOOTS

 and look at

ISA   BENNY

the .

CAMERA

Say " ![] !"

CHEESE

likes to swing

through the .

 likes to swing

through the too!

BABY JAGUAR likes to play

in the **FLOWERS** .

Say " **CHEESE** !"

Here is an cart.
ICE-CREAM

 loves !
BOOTS · ICE CREAM

Say "!"
CHEESE

Uh-oh. Do you see someone behind the cart?

ICE-CREAM

It is !
SWIPER

 wants to swipe
SWIPER

our .
CAMERA

We have to stop .

SWIPER

Say " , no swiping!"

SWIPER

Yay! We stopped !

SWIPER

Hey, there is ! !

TICO

TICO will give us a ride
to the TREE HOUSE in his CAR.
Say " CHEESE !"

Hooray! We made it to the .

TREE HOUSE

And loves all the

BOOTS

pictures!

We cheered up  .
BOOTS
Thanks for helping!

Oh, I have to take **1**
ONE

more picture.

 wants a picture of
BOOTS

you!

Say " ![] !"
CHEESE